FIERCE,
FEARLESS
AND FREE

BLOOMSBURY EDUCATION
Bloomsbury Publishing Plc
50 Bedford Square, London, WC1B 3DP, UK

BLOOMSBURY, BLOOMSBURY EDUCATION and the Diana logo are trademarks of
Bloomsbury Publishing Plc

First published in Great Britain in 2020 by Bloomsbury Publishing Plc
Text copyright © Lari Don, 2020
Illustrations copyright © Eilidh Muldoon, 2020

A catalogue record for this book is available from the British Library

ISBN: PB: 978-1-4729-6713-8; ePDF: 978-1-4729-6710-7; ePub: 978-1-4729-6711-4

2 4 6 8 10 9 7 5 3 1

Typeset by Newgen KnowledgeWorks Pvt. Ltd., Chennai, India
Printed and bound by CPI (UK) Ltd, Croydon, CR0 4YY

To find out more about our authors and books visit www.bloomsbury.com
and sign up for our newsletters

FIERCE, FEARLESS AND FREE

Girls in Myths and Legends from Around the World

Retold by LARI DON

Illustrated by EILIDH MULDOON

BLOOMSBURY EDUCATION
LONDON OXFORD NEW YORK NEW DELHI SYDNEY

*To Ailsa Dixon, an inspiring young storyteller:
keep carrying the flame forward, in your
own wonderful way!*

CONTENTS

KANDEK AND THE WOLF

ARMENIAN FOLK TALE

Once upon a time, a girl called Kandek lived beside a dark dangerous forest.

She often took lunch to her father as he worked in the fields on the edge of the forest. One day, on her way home, she stopped to eat her own lunch: bread, cheese and a crunchy red apple. She sat on a tree stump and bit into the apple.

'I smell something sweet,' said a hoarse voice. 'I smell something sweet and fresh and tasty!'

Kandek looked into the forest and saw an old woman standing in the shadows.

This wasn't a little old lady with fluffy white hair and a sweet smile. This was a tall long-limbed old woman with thick silver-grey hair, a toothy grin, a long nose and yellow nails on her bent fingers and bare toes.

The old woman stared at the hand holding the apple. 'I'm hungry.'

Kandek knew, from listening to her mother's fairy tales, that it was wise to be polite and generous to anyone you met on the edge of the forest. So she walked over to the old woman and offered her the red apple.

The old woman grabbed Kandek's wrist. 'I don't want to eat the apple. I want to eat *you*!'

Just for a moment, the old woman's nose lengthened into a snout, her teeth grew sharper, and her bare feet sprouted grey fur and curved claws.

Kandek had been polite and generous... to a werewolf.

Now the werewolf was holding her tight.

The old woman laughed, threw Kandek into a sack, tied the top of the sack and lifted it on to her back. Then she strode through the trees, heading for the depths of the forest.

'You'll boil down into a tender tasty stew for my supper.'

Kandek didn't want to be eaten, by a wolf or an old woman. But she didn't have a knife to slice her way out of the sack. She would have to cut herself free using words.

She moaned, 'I'm so squished in this sack, my muscles are cramped. Let me stretch my legs, or I'll be chewy and stringy rather than tender and tasty.'

The old woman dropped the sack on the ground and untied it. 'Stretch your legs,' she snapped. 'But be quick.'

Kandek clambered out. She pointed and circled her left foot. She pointed and circled her right foot. Then she said, 'Of course, the best way to stretch your legs is to... RUN!'

Kandek sprinted towards the edge of the forest.

As she ran, she thought: that old woman will never catch me.

But the old woman didn't stay an old woman. She shifted, completely and suddenly, into a wolf. A long-legged, silver-furred wolf.

The wolf ran after Kandek.

Kandek sprinted as fast as she could. But the wolf was faster.

Kandek could see green fields through the trees; she was nearly out of the forest. Then the wolf leaped at her, landed on her shoulders and knocked her to the ground.

The werewolf had caught her prey again.

The silver wolf gripped one of Kandek's boots in her jaws and dragged the girl back to the sack. The old woman shoved Kandek inside again, tied it up again and carried her through the forest again.

But Kandek didn't give up. She kept trying to open that sack with words. 'I'm getting pins and needles. I'll taste sharp and bitter, unless you let me out.'

'I'll eat you whatever you taste like,' said the old woman.

'This sack smells of salt. Aah-aah-aah-chooo! It's making me sneeze. Aah-aah-aah-chooo! I'll get the inside of your sack all snotty, if you don't let me out.'

'I have other sacks at home,' muttered the old woman.

'I need the toilet! I'm desperate! If you don't let me out, I'll get your sack all wet and smelly.'

The old woman laughed. 'I don't care! I have plenty of other sacks at home.'

They reached the old woman's cottage and she dropped the sack on the hard floor.

Trapped inside the dark salty sack, Kandek heard the old woman stack logs and light a fire. Kandek heard the crackle of flames. Kandek heard the old woman fill a pot with water. Kandek heard the water bubble over the fire.

Kandek did not want to go into that water, over those flames.

She had just one more chance to escape.

Kandek wriggled inside the sack until her feet were flat against the floor, then she tensed her muscles and got ready to spring.

When the old woman untied the sack, Kandek leaped out.

She leaped on to the old woman's shoulders, jumped as high as she could and grabbed one of the rafters holding up the roof. Kandek pulled herself on to the smoke-stained beam and sat there, high above the cottage floor.

Kandek looked down. This was like her own cottage, with firewood drying against the walls, sacks heaped in one corner and a spinning wheel in another. But her family's cottage didn't have an angry silver wolf snarling in the middle of the floor.

'You can't get me!' laughed Kandek. 'Wolves can't climb, or fly!'

The wolf jumped and snapped, and howled and growled, and jumped again. Kandek pulled her feet up on to the rafter and the wolf couldn't reach her.

The wolf shifted into the old woman. 'Wolves can't climb, but I can, if I build a staircase.'

The old woman piled all the logs in the cottage into a pyramid. She started to climb towards the rafters, muttering about dragging Kandek down into the pot.

But the logs were roughly chopped, with sharp edges and splinters. The old woman's bare feet were cut by her firewood staircase. She whined in pain, hopping and jumping as the splinters stabbed her feet. The pile of logs wobbled, then slipped, then rolled. The old woman fell and landed on the floor beside the fire.

She looked around for something else to build a stairway to her supper.

But Kandek already knew the best building material. She pointed to the heap of sacks. Full versions of the empty sack she'd been carried in. Sacks she recognised from her own cottage. Sacks of salt, for preserving meat.

'Those sacks would make a strong staircase,' Kandek said loudly. Then she gasped. 'Ooops, me and my big mouth! Why did I give you such a good idea...?'

The old woman laughed, then hauled the sacks over and piled them up. Soon she had a stable mound of sacks, leading right up to Kandek.

She stepped on to the first sack, then the second, leaving bloody footprints as she climbed.

The salt from the sacks seeped into the cuts from the firewood. And salt in wounds is very painful.

The old woman howled. 'Ow Ow OW!' She hopped and danced. She tried to keep climbing as she hopped, but the pain in her feet was too much. She wobbled and slipped and tumbled and fell...

Right into the pot of water.

As the old woman splashed and spluttered, Kandek swung down from the rafter, slid down the sacks and ran out of the cottage.

Behind her, she heard the howls of the werewolf trying to scramble out of the boiling water. Kandek didn't look back, she just ran through the trees and out of the forest to home and to safety.

I don't know whether the werewolf escaped from the pot, but I do know that neither the silver wolf nor the old woman ever chased Kandek again.

I also know that the next time Kandek met someone she didn't know on the edge of the forest, she was still polite and generous, but she *threw* them an apple, rather than handing it to them. Because Kandek knew that keeping her distance was the safest way to share her lunch, without becoming someone else's supper...

GODDESS VS MOUNTAIN

SUMERIAN MYTH

Inanna enjoyed her job. Both her jobs.

She was Goddess of Love, which meant people sang songs to her, wrote poetry about her, asked for her help to love and be loved, built temples to her and gave her lots of gifts.

She was also Goddess of War, which meant people carried her banners into battle, chanted her name, asked for her help to kill and not be killed, built temples to her and gave her lots of gifts.

She danced to the songs, she admired the banners, she put up with the poetry. She enjoyed the gifts and the worship in the temples. She loved the way people bowed to her: kneeling down and touching their faces to the ground. It showed respect for her power. Also, most people looked silly with their nose to the ground and their bottom in the air.

So Inanna, Goddess of Love and War, loved both her jobs.

Every day, she flew over the land of Sumer in a chariot pulled by six blue bulls, swooping over the Euphrates and Tigris rivers, visiting her temples, watching battles, blessing weddings.

One day, as she soared over Sumer, she noticed something new.

A blot on the horizon.

A dark stain on her perfect world.

Inanna flicked the reins and her bulls flew towards the smudge of dirt on the sky. Soon, Inanna could see it was a mountain. Bigger than any mountain she'd seen before. Much bigger than any mountain she'd seen in this land before.

She guided her bulls into a wide circle round the new mountain, avoiding the smoke pouring from the summit, and she called out, 'I am Inanna.'

The mountain shrugged.

'I am Inanna, Goddess of Love.'

The mountain burped.

'I am Inanna, Goddess of War.'

The mountain farted.

'I am Inanna, Goddess of Love and War, and I demand your respect.'

The mountain spoke. 'I am Ebih, and I am bigger and stronger than you.'

Suddenly a pillar of flame rose from the mountain. The blast of heat burned Inanna's fingers on the reins and scorched her bulls' blue hides.

Inanna steered the chariot into a wider circle, slightly further from the mountain and his flames.

'I am Ebih!' he roared. 'You should show ME respect!'

'You are earthbound and solid; I am made of moonlight and worship. You are a rock; I am a goddess. You will bow down to me!'

'I bow to NO ONE,' bellowed Ebih.

'You will bow to me. You will press your forehead to the earth and rub your nose in the dust.'

'I shake the earth. I create the dust. I am the power in this land now. The people sing to you, but they RUN from me. I am more powerful than any god. You should bow to me, little goddess!'

Ebih roared even louder. Hot rocks shot from his mouth towards the chariot.

Inanna flicked the reins and her bulls flew away from the mountain.

'I'll be back,' she yelled over her shoulder. 'I'll be back with all the gods, then you will bow down!'

As her bulls galloped through the air, Inanna saw that the land around the new mountain was burnt and desolate. Plants were dying from too much smoke and not enough sunlight. People and animals were running from the growing circle of ash and devastation.

Inanna flew home to the palace of the gods, high in the sky. As she leaped off her chariot and unharnessed her bulls, she realised she had ash on her fingers and her skirts were singed. She dashed to her chambers, washed quickly and dressed in her finest robes. She put stars on her forehead and brushed moonbeams into her hair.

Then Inanna strode into the throne room and bowed to Anu, chief of all the gods. 'My lord, there's a new mountain.'

'There are always new mountains.' Anu smiled at her. 'The world is making itself around us, inspired by our power and majesty.'

'This new mountain didn't bow down to me.'

Anu stroked his long black curled beard. 'Maybe he didn't know who you are.'

'He knew. He called me "little goddess". He said he was more powerful than any god.'

Anu walked to the wide windows of the palace, which looked out over the known world.

Anu saw the smoke and leaping fire.

'He's called Ebih,' said Inanna quietly. 'And he didn't show me respect. Let me lead all the gods to the mountain. If Ebih refuses to show us proper respect, we can defeat him together and force him to bow down before us.'

Anu frowned. 'That mountain is far away. It may be wise to recognise the limits of our power. It may be sensible to allow the mountain his own sphere of influence–'

'But Anu, he's destroying the land. He's burning people out of their homes and animals out of their fields. We must force him to bow to us and respect us, then we can order him to stop burping smoke and farting flames.'

'The fire will not reach us here; the smoke will usually blow the other way. We'll be safe in our palace.'

'The people won't be safe. These people pray to us, they make offerings to us, they show us respect. We owe them our protection.'

'The people running from that mountain are showing good sense and an instinct for survival. You should do the same, Inanna.'

'So you won't challenge Ebih?'

Anu shook his head. 'Power recognises power. The gods will leave that mountain alone.'

Inanna clenched her fists. 'I will make him respect me. Because without respect, the gods are nothing.' She ran out of the throne room.

Anu sighed and wondered which of his other nieces and nephews could handle the jobs of love and war, if Inanna didn't return...

In her chambers, the Goddess of Love took off her shining jewels and elegant robes.

Then the Goddess of War dressed for battle.

She chose her favourite bow and arrows, her most accurate spear and lance, her heaviest mace, her sharpest axe and her longest sword. She harnessed her blue bulls, jumped into her chariot and left the palace of the gods. She flew over the dusty dying earth, to circle round the summit of the mountain.

'I am Inanna and you will bow down to me. You will bend your rocky back, press your stony face on the ground and rub your pebbly nose in the dirt. You will show me respect. Then you will leave my land and my people alone.'

'No!' roared Ebih. 'I am the power here. You will bow to me, little goddess.'

'Little goddess?' Inanna smiled, a fierce reckless smile. 'I am the Goddess of WAR!' Then she attacked the mountain.

Standing steady in her chariot, Inanna lifted her bow. She aimed carefully and fired one arrow, then another, then another. She shot all her long sharp arrows into the wide-open mouth of the mountain.

Every arrow reached its target.

And every arrow burned in the heat of the mountain's fire.

'Foolish goddess!' called Ebih. 'Your weapons feed my fire and increase my power.'

Inanna balanced her spear perfectly in her expert grip and threw it at Ebih's wide back. The spear hit the spine of the mountain, but the blade broke on the rock.

She grabbed her mace, her brutal war-hammer, and hurled it at the ribs of the mountain. She grinned when she heard the harsh crunch of impact, then frowned when she saw that her mace had shattered and the mountain was still whole.

She picked up her double-bladed axe, whirled it round her head and flung it at Ebih's skull. But the axe bounced off a cliff face and clattered down to the feet of the mountain.

'Is that all you have, little goddess?'

Inanna screamed in frustration, seized her long lance and aimed it at her enemy's belly.

Then she leaped off the chariot.

The tip of the lance cut through the smoky air, as Inanna forced it in a straight line towards Ebih. The vicious point struck the mountain's flank, hard and true. But the lance split and splintered in Inanna's fist.

The goddess crashed into the side of the mountain.

Inanna lay on the hot stony slope, winded and bruised.

'Have you come to worship me, little goddess?' rumbled Ebih.

Inanna scrambled to her feet. She'd broken almost all her weapons on this arrogant insulting mountain, but she still had her sword.

She sprinted to the top of the mountain, she stood tall and magnificent on his summit, and she called, 'Last chance, Ebih. Bow down to me now or I will drive this sword into your heart!'

'I will not bow down to you, tiny insignificant goddess,' bellowed Ebih. 'I contain the mighty power of the earth and I demand your respect.'

'You will get nothing from me but my blade!' Inanna drove the heaven-sharpened sword deep into the heart of the mountain.

She yelled in triumph as her last blade finally penetrated the mountain's ash-grey skin.

Then she felt the sword get lighter and lighter, as the heat of the mountain melted the blade. The sword was swallowed by Ebih, and Inanna was left holding a warm misshapen hilt.

She stood alone and weaponless on the summit of the hot smoking mountain.

Ebih laughed at her. He chuckled and sniggered and chortled. Vast amused tremors rippled across his rocky ribcage.

The mountain laughed at the goddess.

Inanna watched small stones rattle loose and big boulders roll down his sides as he laughed. She looked up at the sky, towards the palace of the gods. No one was coming to help her.

As Ebih's giggles shook the ground under her feet, Inanna ran down the mountain.

Ebih laughed louder. 'Run away, little goddess!'

But Inanna wasn't running away. She was finding new weapons.

Inanna chased the stones rolling down the slopes. She caught two jagged rocks, lifted them above her head and smashed them into the side of the mountain.

She crashed them into Ebih's stony skin, bashing and battering and bruising the mountain with his own rocks.

She fought Ebih with his own solid stony power.

Inanna used all her strength to hit again and again and again.

She didn't stop when her first two weapons crumbled, because the mountain had laughed so hard that there were lots of rocks lying loose at his feet. Perfect weapons, given to her by the mountain himself.

Inanna picked up more stones and she struck the mountain's ribs and ridges, spine and slopes, cliff faces and crevices.

She used the mountain's strength against him, until the mountain began to bleed.

Until dribbles of red-hot rock seeped from narrow cracks. Until streams of the mountain's blood flowed from deep gullies. Until rivers of the mountain's life poured from long valleys.

Until Ebih croaked and gasped.

Then Inanna stopped, waiting for the mountain to surrender. Waiting for him to promise he would leave her land and people alone. Waiting for him to offer her proper respect.

Waiting for her chance to show him mercy.

But Ebih spat a dribble of molten rock at her.

Inanna sidestepped his final insult. She dropped the rocks, she laid her hands on his warm grey skin, she gripped his thick grey bones and she wrestled the mountain to the ground.

Then the goddess stood on top of a cold grey heap of rubble, her arms raised in triumph.

The clouds of smoke drifted away.

The layer of ash blew off the land.

The people returned home.

The people thanked Inanna. They bowed down, pressing their foreheads to the ground and wiping their noses on the earth. The people brought her gifts, and sang about their love and respect for her.

And the people built a temple to Inanna, on top of the rocky mound that had once been Ebih.

They built a temple so huge and glittering that it was visible from Anu's throne room. A temple so splendid that no one could ever forget, on earth or in the palace of the gods, that Inanna had defeated a mountain.

NERINGA AND THE
SEA DRAGON

LITHUANIAN LEGEND

One day, a fisherman found a baby floating in a basket on the sea. It was a big basket, containing a big bouncy baby girl, who waved at him cheerfully when he lifted her out of the water.

He took the baby home, called her Neringa and brought her up as his daughter. Neringa grew into a happy healthy toddler. She grew, and she grew, and she grew. And she kept growing.

Because Neringa was a giant.

By the time Neringa was a year old, she was taller than her dad. By the time she was five years old, she was taller than their cottage, and had to move her bed into the boat shed. By the time she was ten years old, she was taller than the masts of the fishing boats in the harbour.

Despite her size, Neringa fitted in well to the life of the fishing village. She was kind and thoughtful and never got annoyed when she was the first person found in games of hide-and-seek. (It's hard to hide when you're a giant...)

She used her size and strength to help her family, friends and neighbours. She was tall enough to spot boats returning from the open sea long before anyone else. She was strong enough to lift boats out of the harbour for repairs. Her apron was big enough to carry everyone's catch to market.

When Neringa finally stopped growing, twenty years after her father adopted her, she was the most beautiful giant in the land. She had long golden hair, shinier than the sand on the shore; she had clear blue eyes, brighter than the sea in the sunlight; and most importantly she had a cheerful smile.

Tales of this beautiful young giant spread across the land and across the sea.

The sea dragon Naglis heard the stories, on his rocky island out in the ocean.

Naglis was a huge beast, scaly and stinky and cruel. He was struggling to find a bride, because he'd accidentally trampled on, or inadvertently swallowed, all his previous wives.

'But I didn't notice her under my claws!' he whined. 'They're all so small! I need someone my own size...'

When he heard rumours of a pretty young giant living in a village on the coast, Naglis grinned. 'She sounds perfect! I'm sure she'd love to be my wife.'

The sea dragon polished his claws, sharpened his teeth, waxed his scales, then set off to ask Neringa to marry him.

Neringa was sitting on the harbour wall, holding up a large net so the fishermen could check it for rips, when Naglis reared out of the sea.

The dragon boomed, 'Neringa, will you marry me and live with me on my rocky island?'

Neringa lowered the net and looked at Naglis. He was a muddy sort of grey colour, with sharp unwelcoming scales, small unfriendly eyes and long brown teeth.

Also, he was a dragon.

'No, thank you,' she said politely. 'It's kind of you to ask, but I would prefer to stay here.'

The dragon sneered at the fisherfolk, at their salt-stained clothes and little cottages. 'But everything is so *small*. Why would you want to stay here?'

Neringa smiled. 'Because my family, friends and neighbours live here. This is my home.' She held the net up again.

The dragon wasn't used to anyone saying 'no' to him.

'Say yes to me,' he roared, 'or I will make you sorry!'

'No. Thank you.'

'Then I will wreck the boats of your family and friends and neighbours!' Naglis smashed his tail on the surface of the sea. A huge wave swept inland and the boats in the harbour were thrown on to the front street of the village.

'Witness the power of Naglis the sea dragon!' he bellowed. 'Will you marry me NOW?'

'No, I will not.' Neringa picked up the boats and put them carefully back in the water, then she sat cross-legged on the beach and started to repair the broken masts.

The dragon swam off in a huff.

But he didn't give up. The next morning, when the fishermen sailed out to sea, the dragon rose up out of the depths and overturned one of the boats. As it sank, the other fishermen pulled their neighbours out of the waves, then took them safely home.

Naglis followed them to the harbour. He roared at Neringa, 'If you don't marry me, I will sink all the boats.'

Neringa stood on the harbour wall and called back, 'I will not marry you, so go away and leave this village alone.'

'How dare you refuse me! If you don't say yes, I will destroy your precious village.'

'I will never say yes and I will not let you destroy my home.' Neringa stood tall and strong, with cottages lined up like toys behind her. She folded her arms and stared at the dragon.

So Naglis called up a storm. He focused all his sea-dragon power and fury, and forced howling winds towards the village.

The wind whipped the sea into high foamy walls of heavy water, which crushed the boats then rushed up the shore towards the cottages and the people inside.

The fisherfolk ran inland for safety, Neringa carrying the smallest children in her arms.

They watched the dragon's storm batter their harbour and their homes. When the wind and waves finally died down, they walked slowly back to the village. All their boats were wrecked or sunk; all their cottages were roofless and sodden.

Neringa strode out past the shattered harbour wall, wading fearlessly through the open sea towards the dragon. She shouted, 'Naglis, hear me. I will never marry you. And you will never harm this village again.'

Naglis heard the anger in the giant's voice, he saw the strength in her long strides and the power in her clenched fists.

He gulped and swam further out to sea. 'I'll wait here. You'll change your mind soon, when your friends starve because my tail sinks every boat that tries to fish, when your neighbours freeze because my storms rip off every roof they try to build.'

Neringa shook her head. 'You can wait there as long as you like, but you'll never harm my friends or neighbours again.'

Neringa turned her back on the dragon and walked along the shoreline, filling her apron with rocks and sand. Then she walked back out to sea and laid the rocks in a smooth curving line. She laid golden sand on top, forming a wall in the ocean. For a whole day the giant carried rocks and sand out to sea, building a high golden wall between her home and the dragon, creating a calm lagoon in front of her village.

She didn't cut the village off from the sea completely; she left a small channel out to the open water, so fish could swim into the lagoon and fishermen could fill their nets. But the channel was too narrow for the dragon or his storms to get past the curved golden wall.

Naglis the sea dragon realised he was beaten, by Neringa's determination, her strength and her love for her village. So he swam back to his lonely rocky island.

Neringa helped her family, friends and neighbours rebuild their homes and their boats, then they all fished safely and happily for many years to come.

And you can visit that long golden wall of sand. It's the beautiful Curonian peninsula in Lithuania, where the locals still tell stories about the giant who built a wall in the sea to protect them from a dragon.

KATE CRACKERNUTS
AND THE
SHEEP-HEADED MONSTER

SCOTTISH FAIRY TALE

K ate woke up one morning to find a monster weeping in her bedroom.

Kate lived in the palace, because her mother had married the king a few years ago. So Kate was used to tournaments and masked balls. But she wasn't used to monsters sobbing in her bedroom.

And this was a particularly horrible monster. With long curving horns, eerie yellow eyes, greasy wool covering its heavy head, and snot dangling down on to its lacy blue nightgown.

A blue nightgown that looked exactly like her stepsister Ann's favourite nightgown.

Kate loved her stepsister Ann, who was the king's daughter and would be queen one day. Suddenly Kate wasn't scared for herself. Suddenly she was scared for Ann.

Why was this monster wearing Ann's nightie? Had this monster stolen Ann's clothes? Had it hurt Ann?

Had it *eaten* Ann?

Furious and frightened, Kate leaped out of bed, grabbed her slippers and whacked the monster with them.

The monster didn't fight Kate or even defend itself. The monster backed off, taking quick small steps away from Kate, almost like it was dancing.

Kate looked down, and realised the monster was wearing slippers. Embroidered silver slippers, just like her own slippers, on pale soft feet.

Those feet didn't look monstrous.

Kate stopped whacking the monster and stared at it.

From the toes up to the neck, this monster looked exactly like her sister. But on the trembling shoulders, instead of Ann's curly ginger head, there was a greasy horned sheep's head.

'Ann? Is that you?'

The sheep-headed monster nodded.

'Oh, Ann! Who did this to you?'

'I did,' said Kate's mother, as she opened the door. 'I bargained for a fairy spell to turn a princess into a monster. Wasn't it a good idea? She can't possibly be queen now, so I'm sure your stepfather will name you his heir instead.'

'That's a terrible idea!' said Kate. 'I don't want Ann to be a monster, just so I can be queen. Turn her back, now!'

Her mother shrugged. 'I can't turn her back. I only bargained for one spell, so she's stuck with that sheep's head forever.' Kate's mother smiled regally and left the room.

Ann sat down on the floor, sniffling and snorting through her woolly nose.

'Don't worry,' said Kate. 'I'll find a way to lift the spell.'

Kate packed a bag with a couple of bannocks, a handful of hazelnuts and an iron nail. She kissed her sheep-headed sister goodbye and headed into the woods to search for a bright green grassy mound and listen for beautiful music.

She walked all day long, cracking open nuts and nibbling bannocks when she was hungry. As the sun was setting, she found a perfect bright green mound and heard the joyful sound of pipes and fiddles.

Kate sat down to wait.

Soon, a young man skipped and stumbled towards the mound, calling, 'Open up for the dancing prince!'

The grass slid open to form an elegant archway. The young man stumbled and skipped inside. Kate followed, sticking the iron nail into the grassy arch as she ran through, so it wouldn't close behind her.

She found herself in a splendid ballroom, with musicians performing at one end, beautiful people dancing in the centre, and gorgeous people sitting at tables round the edges, with toddlers and children playing at their feet.

The silks and velvets were brighter than anything at her stepfather's palace, the dancing was faster and more intricate, the music was more enticing, the smiles were more glorious...

Kate had found the fairies.

She hid in the shadows against the wall. She wanted to dance to the wonderful music, but she resisted the temptation and stayed in the shadows.

Kate crept nearer to two fairy women sitting at the tables, who were laughing and chatting and pointing at the dancers.

'That handsome prince has been here every night for weeks, dancing his life away. His family have no idea that three feathers from my babe's golden hen would break the spell and save his life!'

Kate looked under the table. All the children were playing with toys or animals. One girl had a leafy twig, another had a silver hare; one boy had a black flute, another had a golden hen.

She looked at the prince, whirling in the centre of the floor. He was pale and thin. And he was going to die soon, if he didn't stop dancing with the fairies.

She sighed, then crawled under the table and rolled a couple of hazelnuts towards the fairy boy with the golden hen. He let go of the bird to grab the nuts.

Kate picked up the hen and shoved it inside her cloak. She stayed under the table and tried to ignore the tempting music, concentrating on the conversation above her.

The fairy women gossiped and giggled about glamour spells and love potions, but neither of them mentioned a sheep-headed princess.

Kate was sure these fairies knew how to break Ann's spell, but she had to stay hidden and wait for them to discuss it. If she stood up and asked them directly, they might cast a spell on her too.

She crouched under the table and listened as they laughed and chatted about changelings and fairy flags, but they didn't mention how to lift a sheep's head spell.

The night was passing, the dancers were slowing, the youngest children under the tables were dozing.

Kate was running out of time to save her sister.

She crawled closer to the fairy children and whispered, 'I wonder if any of you can make animal noises. Who can make the sound of a sheep?'

They all grinned and opened their mouths. 'Baa baa, meh meh, baa baaa baaaaa!'

They were almost as loud as the dance music and not nearly as tuneful.

The fairy women above laughed and one of them said, 'That reminds me of the sheep-headed monster spell we gave that scheming queen. The poor woolly princess has no idea that tapping her horns three times with my babe's willow wand would break her spell.'

Kate grinned and rolled her last three hazelnuts towards the fairy girl with the leafy twig. The little girl dropped the stick to pick up the nuts.

Kate grabbed the willow wand and put it safely under her cloak. Then she crept out from under the table. She was so keen to get home and free her sister from the spell, she didn't even glance back at the dancing prince.

She walked through the archway, pulled out the iron nail and ran through the dark woods.

The sun was rising as she sprinted into her room, where Ann was embroidering slippers by the fire.

Kate tapped the sheep's horns three times with the willow wand, there was a smell of burning wool, and suddenly Ann was standing in front of her with a big smile on her entirely human face.

The sisters hugged each other.

There was a startled squawk.

Ann laughed. 'Why do you have a hen under your cloak?'

Kate grinned. 'So I can save a prince. But first, let's go down for breakfast and see what my mother says when she sees you without wool and horns!'

And that's how Kate used a handful of hazelnuts to rescue her sister, save a prince and win herself the name Kate Crackernuts.

RIINA AND THE RED STONE AXE

SOLOMON ISLANDS FOLK TALE

This is the story of three islands, in an ocean of thousands of islands. It's the story of a large island where hundreds of happy families lived, fished and enjoyed feasts together; a medium-sized island where dozens of fierce warrior women trained together; and a small island where two cannibal brothers lived together in a cave lined with skulls.

The cannibal brothers owned magic axes which gave them great strength and the power to fly. One day they were flying across the large island, after enjoying a village feast. They saw two girls walking along a path, so they swooped down, grabbed the girls and flew to their small island.

The cannibals dropped the girls on the ground outside their filthy bone-filled cave.

The cannibal brothers stared at the girls.

The girls trembled.

The cannibal brothers licked their lips.

The girls shivered.

The cannibals laughed. 'We're not hungry, because we just feasted on a whole village. We won't eat you; we'll keep you as our servants.'

The girls started work, cleaning the cave.

But the girls refused to eat the food the cannibals brought them. They refused to eat human flesh. They even refused to eat brains, which the brothers said was the tastiest bit.

The brothers allowed the girls time off to fish, in order to feed themselves. So the girls could go down to the beach on their own, but they couldn't escape, because there were no canoes on the island. The brothers didn't own any boats, because they could fly from island to island.

The girls worked hard, cleaning the cannibals' cave and sharpening the cannibals' knives. But they were never allowed to sharpen, or even go near, the cannibals' two red stone axes.

The girls' final job at the end of every day was to display any new skulls on rock ledges lining the cave walls. One day the cannibals brought two of the girls' neighbours home to eat. That evening, the girls folded their arms, shook their heads and refused to display the new skulls.

One brother muttered, 'These servants are more trouble than they're worth. They're picky eaters, they need time off to catch and cook disgusting fish, now they're refusing to put skulls on our souvenir shelves.'

The other brother nodded. 'Perhaps it's time to eat them?'

But the girls' families had heard rumours, whispers on the waves, that the cannibals had two new female servants. The families hoped the servants were their own stolen girls, so they offered a huge reward – betel-nut trees, porpoise teeth, tusked pigs and strings of shell money – to whoever rescued their daughters.

A fleet of one hundred canoes, rowed by lots of strong young men, set off to rescue the girls. When the one hundred canoes reached the small island, the cannibals laughed. 'Our food is delivering itself!'

The brothers ate a huge feast that day. The girls spent all night displaying fresh new skulls. Only a handful of the one hundred canoes and their warriors escaped to return home.

The whispering waves carried word of the huge reward to the island of the warrior women. Their fearless leader, Riina, decided she would rescue the girls.

Riina navigated just one canoe, rowed by her warriors, towards the cannibals' island.

When they got near the shore, Riina ordered her warrior women to lie down flat in the bottom of the canoe, so they were hidden. Riina stood up tall and straight, so she could be seen from the island.

The brothers watched a lone woman float towards the shore.

One brother grinned. 'Another snack, coming straight to us!'

He picked up his axe and flew to the canoe to grab Riina. He swooped down, reaching for her throat.

But the warrior was faster than the cannibal. Riina grabbed his hair and flung him into the bottom of the canoe.

When he crash-landed, he let go of his red stone axe.

And Riina stepped over the axe.

It was taboo – in those islands, in those days – for a woman to step over a sacred object. When Riina stepped over the sacred red stone axe, all the power drained from the axe. When his axe become powerless, so did the cannibal. Suddenly he had no strength and no power to fly.

He couldn't fight off the warriors as they tied him up in the bottom of the canoe.

Riina and her band of women rowed to the beach and leaped out, dragging the bound cannibal with them.

'Let my brother go!' screamed the other cannibal. He flew out of the cave towards the warriors, ready to slash and bite and kill.

Riina threw her favourite boomerang towards the cannibal's hand. Her perfect aim knocked his red stone axe from his fingers. It hit the ground and one of the other women warriors stepped over it.

The sacred axe lost its power, so the second cannibal fell out of the air and crashed on to the sand.

As soon as both brothers were powerless, the two girls ran from the skull-lined cave and jumped into the canoe. Riina and her warriors rowed them away, towards safety and freedom, leaving the cannibals on the beach.

The girls were welcomed home with a huge feast. Riina was given the huge reward.

And the two cannibals were trapped on an island with no power to fly and no canoes. I wonder if they ever learned to catch and eat fish?

MEDEA AND THE METAL MAN

GREEK MYTH

This is the story of an ancient getaway after a mythical robbery.

Jason, his companions the Argonauts, the Golden Fleece they'd just stolen from the king of Colchis, and the girl who'd helped them steal it, were all sailing from Colchis to Greece on Jason's ship the *Argo*. They were running out of fresh water, having left the scene of the crime in a bit of a hurry, so Jason decided to land on an island to stock up.

The nearest island was Crete. But Crete was guarded by the first robot in history. (The first robot in mythology, at least.)

Hephaestus, the god of metalwork, had forged a giant man out of gleaming sheets of bronze. This huge metal warrior was called Talos and he was powered by ichor: the golden blood of the gods. Hephaestus had filled Talos's single vein by pouring ichor through a hole in Talos's left ankle and he'd stoppered the hole with a tight-fitting iron nail. Then the god had given the robot to the people of Crete.

Talos's job was to guard Crete by patrolling the island's shores. The giant metal man ran round the shoreline three times every day, watching for invaders. If he saw an invading ship, it was his duty to throw rocks at it until it sank or sailed away.

But the first-ever robot was starting to malfunction. Perhaps Talos was overdue a service. Perhaps a cog or wheel had come loose. Whatever the reason, he no longer just attacked invaders, he now threw rocks at every ship that came close, driving traders and travellers and tourists away from Crete.

So when the *Argo* sailed near the coast, Talos threw rocks at it.

The Argonauts were expert sailors and they dodged the rocks flying towards them by tacking and swerving, zigging and zagging. But they couldn't keep that up forever and they still needed to reach land, because they were all thirsty.

'We come in peace!' shouted Jason. 'We just want fresh water. Please, shiny metal man, let us land.'

'No one may land on my island,' Talos yelled back. 'Sail away or I will sink you!'

He threw another rock and the *Argo* jerked out of the way again.

'Let me deal with this metal monster,' said Orpheus, whose magical music had lulled the king's guard dragon to sleep so Jason could sneak past to steal the Golden Fleece.

As Orpheus tuned his lyre, the girl watched, leaning against the mast and shaking her head.

When Orpheus started to play, the Argonauts put wax in their ears so they couldn't hear his dangerous music. But Talos couldn't hear it either, past the splashing of rocks landing in the sea. He heard occasional notes, but not enough of the beautiful lullaby to make him sleepy.

So the rocks kept flying towards the ship.

Orpheus put down his lyre, the Argonauts unplugged their ears and Jason said, 'Let's do this the traditional way. Let's just kill him.'

The girl leaning against the mast smiled, and shook her head again.

A handful of Argonauts kept steering and sailing the ship; the rest picked up their spears and bows and arrows, and aimed at the burnished bronze heart of Talos.

Even though the ship was jerking and tacking to avoid the rocks, the Argonauts were all excellent warriors, so they hit their shiny target every single time. But their spear-points and arrowheads just made a small *ting* noise as they struck the robot's metal skin, then fell to the ground. Talos was too well made to be damaged by such tiny weapons.

And the rocks kept flying towards the ship.

'Stop wasting your arrows!' said the girl, whose name was Medea.

Medea had helped Jason steal the Golden Fleece from her own father, the king of Colchis. Medea was clever and brave and powerful, but not particularly good at family loyalty.

'Stop wasting your arrows,' said Medea again. 'I'll deal with this metal man.'

'How?' asked Jason. 'You don't have any weapons.'

'I don't need weapons. I just need my words and his weakness.'

'What weakness? I only see strength and size and shiny metal muscles…'

But Medea had already dived off the *Argo* and started swimming to shore.

As she stepped on to the beach, she flicked her wet hair out of her face and saw a huge dark shadow around her on the sand. She rubbed the water out of her eyes. The shadow was getting bigger.

Medea looked up. She saw a massive metal foot crashing down towards her.

She jumped out of the way as the foot thumped on to the beach.

Then the other foot crashed down. She jumped out of the way of that too.

Just like the ship had been zigging and zagging out to sea, Medea had to zig and zag across the beach as Talos stamped his heavy bronze feet down, trying to crush her.

Talos stamped, left right left right…

Medea dodged, right left right left…

And Talos just missed her, every time.

Finally Talos yelled, 'Stand still, small human! Stand still so I can step on you.'

'Why would I do that?' Medea gasped, as she kept running.

'Because I'm going to step on you eventually,' shouted Talos, as he kept stomping. 'So you might as well save us both all this effort. Then I can get back to sinking that sneaky ship.'

But she kept dodging and he kept missing.

'Stand still! It would be a glorious end to anyone's story, to be crushed by the first metal man in history!'

Medea leaped to the right. 'It would be a memorable and heroic way to go, crushed on a golden beach by a bronze robot. Probably better than any other way I'm likely to be remembered. But...'

'But what? Stop dodging, stand still!'

Medea leaped to the left. 'But if that was to be the end of my story, it would have to be a *flawless* metal man who crushed me. Anything else would be embarrassing, not glorious. I can't stand still for you, because you aren't flawless.'

'Of course I'm flawless. I was created by a god. Look at me!' He flexed his bronzed biceps, then crashed his right foot down.

'You're quite impressive, but you do have one small flaw.'

'No, I don't!' He crashed his left foot down, even harder.

Medea dodged out of his way. 'Yes you do! That nail, on your left ankle. It's not bronze, like the rest of you, so it doesn't gleam in the sunlight. That nail is iron, so it's grey and dull and I can even see a spot of rust.'

'*Rust!* Where?'

'On the underside of the nail. I see it every time you try to squash me with your left foot. That's your flaw. That's why it would not be a glorious end to be crushed by you. That's why I won't stand still.'

'If I didn't have that nail in my ankle, you'd stand still?'

'Oh yes. I'm sure I would...'

Talos bent down to pull out the nail. But his bronze fingers were big and the iron nail was small, so he couldn't get a firm grip.

'Would you like some help?' asked Medea.

'Yes, please.'

'Then *you* stand still.'

Talos stood perfectly still, while Medea walked to the giant metal foot which had been trying to crush her. Medea wrapped her hands round the nail (it was tiny to Talos, but huge to Medea) and used all her strength to haul it out.

As the nail slid out, ichor dripped down Talos's gleaming skin. The ichor trickled out, then flowed, then gushed...

Medea stepped away from the fountain of golden blood.

Then she stepped further back, as the huge metal man crashed to the sand.

Once all the ichor had drained out of his single vein, Talos lay still. Empty and hollow. Just a shiny statue lying on a beach.

The *Argo* landed, and the Argonauts cheered Medea back on board, stocked up on water, then sailed away in their getaway ship, with their stolen Golden Fleece.

Once everyone heard that Talos was lying motionless on a Cretan beach, the traders, travellers and tourists could sail to Crete again. All because Medea had noticed the first robot's one small rusty point of weakness.

BRIDGET AND
THE WITCHES

IRISH FOLK TALE

Bridget and her mother knew that their cottage must be clean and tidy before they went to bed. Sweep the floor, wipe the plates, scrub the table, bank the fire, pour out the feetwater, lock the door... Bridget, her mother and all their neighbours did these chores to be virtuous and respectable.

And, of course, to keep the witches out.

Because a house that isn't clean and tidy gives witches the means (and, some would say, the right) to enter overnight.

So every night, Bridget and her mother tidied up, cleaned up, locked up. But one Friday, tired from their day's work in the fields, exhausted from their evening's work spinning and baking, they forgot just one thing.

They forgot to throw the feetwater out the door.

They left the tub of warm water by the fireplace, where they'd soaked their sore feet at the end of a long day.

When Bridget and her mother were falling asleep, there was a scratch at the door and a voice called, 'Feetwater, feetwater, open the door.'

The feetwater sniggered, full of the unruliness of dirt. 'I'd be happy to open the door.'

The feetwater slopped over the side of the tub and slithered in a winding path to the door. The feetwater flowed up the door, flicked the latch and dribbled back to its tub.

The door swung open and in came three witches, with long sharp fingernails, sour creased faces and dusty green cloaks.

The witches stomped over to the fireplace, sat on the stools by the fading warmth, got out their spindles and started to spin.

But they didn't spin their own wool. They grabbed handfuls from the family's bag of wool. They warmed themselves by throwing the family's firewood on the fire. They filled their bellies by chewing on the family's bread and butter.

Bridget and her mother cowered in their narrow bed in the corner of the cottage, hugging each other tight.

'They might not leave,' whispered her mother. 'Now they're inside, they might stay until they've taken all our wool, burned all our firewood and eaten all our food. Then we'll have nothing between us and cold starvation.' She shivered.

'I'll get rid of them,' said Bridget.

She tied her shawl round her shoulders and plaited her hair. As she tidied herself up, she gathered her courage and her wits.

Then she stood up and said, 'Hello, ladies. Can I help you at all?'

All three witches stopped spinning and turned to look at Bridget.

The first witch snarled at her.

The second witch licked her lips and rubbed her belly.

The third witch smiled, showing her sharp teeth. 'No, thank you. We have everything we need.'

'What about a cup of tea? It's thirsty work, spinning, especially beside such a hot fire. And surely you'd like something to wash down all the bread you've been eating. Would you not like a cup of tea, ladies?'

The first witch snarled again, the second witch laughed and the third witch frowned, then nodded. 'Spinning is thirsty work. We would accept a cup of tea.'

Bridget smiled. 'I'll nip out to the well for fresh water. All the water indoors is nasty and dirty and unwholesome.' She glared at the feetwater, then grabbed a bucket. She pushed the door open and ran out to the well.

As she filled the bucket, Bridget looked around her, hoping for inspiration. How could she get rid of the terrifying witches who'd invaded her home? What would make them leave while there was still wool and fuel and food to steal?

She looked up at the hills, lit white and grey by the moonlight. Each hill had a different story. Fionn mac Cumhaill slept under one hill, the fairies danced inside another. The highest hill was called Sliabh na mBan, the hill of the women, and it was rumoured to be the home of the witches.

Bridget would do anything to protect her home. Perhaps the witches felt the same about their home.

So Bridget dropped the bucket with a crash, ran into the cottage and screamed, 'Fire! Flames! Fire! Ruin! Sliabh na mBan is burning! The hill of the women is on fire!'

The three witches leaped up, yelling, 'Our children, our meal chests, our brooms, all burning! Our butter kegs, our wool cards, our hats, all burning!' Then they ran out of the cottage.

Bridget grabbed the tub of feetwater, threw the filthy liquid outside, slammed the door and locked it.

Then she sat beside her mother, who was trembling on the bed.

'How can a hill be on fire?' whispered her mother.

'It's not on fire, Ma, I just said that to get them out the door.'

'When they realise you've tricked them, will they come back, angrier and hungrier than before?'

'Let them come back,' said Bridget. 'They'll not steal any more of our food or wool or warmth, because they won't get through that door.'

'Are you sure?' asked her mother.

Bridget didn't answer.

They both sat, silent and shivering, staring at the locked door.

And they waited.

Then they heard sharp nails scratching.

They heard a harsh voice demand, 'Feetwater, feetwater, open the door!'

And they heard a damp voice whimper, 'How can I open the door? I'm under your feet, soaking into the cold ground. I'm locked out too.'

The three witches stomped off, to look for another house with forgotten feetwater inside.

After that night, Bridget and her mother occasionally forgot to sweep the floor or scrub the table, but they never ever forgot to pour out the feetwater. And the witches from Sliabh na mBan never bothered them again.

PETROSINELLA AND
THE TOWER

ITALIAN FAIRY TALE

Once upon a time, there was a beautiful garden, filled with fruit, flowers, herbs and no weeds at all. This garden was owned and tended by an ogre, who loved the beautiful plants because she couldn't see any beauty in herself. She was taller than the cherry trees in her garden, with skin as green as the leaves on the rosebushes, claws as sharp as the thorns, and teeth as long and yellow as the parsnips in the vegetable patch.

Beside the ogre's garden was a little house, with a window overlooking the herbs and flowers. Inside the house lived a woman who was expecting her first baby. She sat at the window every day, looking down at the gorgeous garden. Like many pregnant women, she had a craving: a desire for one particular thing to eat. A desire so strong that she could think of nothing else.

She didn't crave cherries or apples or pears. She craved the dark green leaves of the parsley growing under her window.

Her craving was stronger than her common sense, so one day, when the ogre went to the village market, the pregnant woman clambered out of her window into the garden. She snipped a sprig of parsley and chewed it.

It tasted amazing! The best parsley she'd ever eaten!

Every day, when the ogre stomped off to market with her basket, the woman clambered out and nibbled just one tiny sprig of parsley, then climbed back into her own little house.

One evening, the ogre decided to make parsley sauce. When she reached the bed of rich brown earth where she grew her crop of parsley, she saw that half the stalks had been cut short and half the leaves were gone.

The next day, instead of going to market, the ogre crouched down and hid behind the fruit trees, waiting to see who was stealing her herbs. The ogre watched the pregnant woman climb out of the window into the garden and cut her precious parsley.

'THIEF!' The ogre leaped out and grabbed the woman's thin white arm in her thick green fingers.

The pregnant woman wept. 'I'm just nibbling one tiny sprig a day, because my baby needs the parsley!'

'I needed that parsley for my sauce,' boomed the ogre. 'By stealing one sprig a day, you've destroyed my crop. If I can't have parsley sauce, maybe I should have neighbour soup. I could boil you up in my soup pot, then use your bones to fertilise my garden.'

The woman wailed. 'Please don't eat me! I'll give you anything you want, if you let me go...'

The ogre smiled. 'If you promise to give me that baby in your belly, when it's old enough not to need milk and nappies, then I'll let you go.'

The woman promised that the ogre could have her child, rather than her life, then left the garden. She never went back, because her craving for parsley wasn't as strong as her fear of the ogre's soup pot.

A few months later, the woman gave birth to a beautiful baby girl, with a full head of glossy rich brown hair and a birthmark in the shape of a parsley leaf on her shoulder. She called the baby Petrosinella.

The baby grew strong and happy, her hair growing even faster than the rest of her.

Soon it was time for little Petrosinella to go to school.

Every day, when she skipped to school, she passed the ogre's garden gate. Every day, when she skipped home, the ogre would say loudly, 'Dear little girl, tell your mother to remember her promise.'

So little Petrosinella would say, 'Mummy! The big green lady next door says to remember your promise!'

Her mother would wipe her eyes and blow her nose, but she never told Petrosinella what the promise was.

One day, the ogre boomed, 'Dear little girl, tell your mother she must keep her promise *tomorrow*!'

Petrosinella skipped indoors. 'Mummy! The big green lady next door says the promise is tomorrow!'

Her mother burst into tears. Then she put her hand on Petrosinella's forehead. 'I think you have a fever. You can't go to school tomorrow, you'll have to stay safely at home.'

The next day, Petrosinella stayed in bed.

The ogre next door watched out for the little girl going to school. When Petrosinella didn't skip past the garden gate, the ogre punched her green fist through the bedroom window and grabbed the little girl.

The ogre stuck Petrosinella under her arm and marched out of the village, with the little girl's long hair trailing on the ground behind them.

The ogre took Petrosinella to a tower she'd built in the dark forest: a tall tower with one wide window at the top and one half-finished doorway at the bottom. The ogre squeezed through the doorway, carried Petrosinella up the stairs and sat her on a soft feathery bed in the room at the top of the tower.

'Your mother made a foolish promise,' said the ogre, 'so this is your home now.'

The ogre stomped back down the stairs, stepped out of the tower and bricked up the doorway.

Now the tower had only one window, and no door at all.

Petrosinella was trapped inside.

She grew up in that tower. She grew taller, her hair grew even longer and she grew more beautiful every day, like the spring flowers in the ogre's garden.

The ogre loved watching Petrosinella bloom into her perfect beauty.

The ogre tried to be kind. She brought tasty food, interesting books and pretty fabric for Petrosinella.

Every evening, the ogre climbed into the tower using Petrosinella's long plaited hair, which Petrosinella wrapped round a hook to take the weight.

Every evening, the ogre stitched new clothes for Petrosinella, cooked her supper, told her tales of the witches who lived in the forest, chatted about what was growing in the garden that week and said that none of the flowers in the garden were as beautiful as the flower in the tower.

Every night, before returning to her garden, the ogre sang Petrosinella to sleep.

The ogre was kind, except for one thing: she refused to let Petrosinella leave the tower.

Petrosinella was determined not to spend the rest of her life in the tower. Every day she tried to escape.

She ran down the winding stairs and tried to find a way out at the base of the tower. But the walls were solid. She ran back up to her room and tried to escape through the window. But the shutters, which were open wide when the ogre climbed in and out, slammed shut every time Petrosinella put her foot on the sill.

There was no way out.

She was trapped.

Even so, she kept trying to escape.

One day, a young prince rode into the forest to hunt. He found the tower with no door and called up, 'Is anyone in there?'

Petrosinella called down, 'Yes! I've been here for ten years and I can't get out!'

'If you let down that long shiny hair, I'll climb up and keep you company in your prison!'

'It's not company I need,' said Petrosinella. 'It's a way out!'

The prince walked round the base of the tower, hunting for a hidden door or a loose stone. Eventually he called up, 'I can't find a way in, but I promise I'll keep trying!'

The prince kept his promise. Every day he returned, with a hammer, a chisel or a crowbar. Every day he tried to break into the tower. Every day he failed. But every day he told Petrosinella stories about the world outside the forest, the world she knew she'd never see unless she escaped from the tower.

Their conversations were loud and cheerful, so Petrosinella always asked the prince to leave long before the ogre visited each evening.

Despite her caution, someone overheard them. A woman who lived nearby, in a little house smelling of vanilla and ginger, heard the prince's deep voice, the girl's light voice and their laughter. She crept closer and listened to them chat about the world outside the forest.

This nosy neighbour had always wanted to bake with the fruit from the ogre's garden, so she decided to tell the ogre what she'd heard. She waited in the shadows at the bottom of the tower until the ogre arrived. The nosy neighbour sidled up to the ogre and whispered, 'Your girl in the tower is talking to *boys*...'

The nosy neighbour told the ogre about the prince, the tools and the conversations. Then she asked, 'Are you worried that your pretty flower might escape?'

'No,' boomed the ogre. 'The tower is enchanted to prevent Petrosinella escaping and the magic is anchored to three acorns hidden inside. She can't escape, unless she takes all three acorns with her. So I'm not worried. But it was neighbourly of you to tell me. Would you like a gift from my garden, as thanks?'

The nosy neighbour grinned. 'I'd love some cherries, to bake cherry pie.'

The ogre nodded, then climbed up Petrosinella's hair.

While they ate supper, the ogre and the girl chatted. The ogre didn't mention the prince, because she knew Petrosinella could never leave the tower. Petrosinella didn't mention that she'd heard every word the ogre had said at the bottom of the tower...

Next day, Petrosinella let down her hair for the prince for the first time. 'Climb up and help me look for three magic acorns.'

Petrosinella found the first acorn, hidden in a knothole in a wooden floorboard. The prince found the second acorn, balanced on a rafter in the roof.

But no matter where they searched – on the shelves, in the wardrobe, under the mattress –

they couldn't find the third acorn. Petrosinella tried to leave with two acorns in her pocket, but the window slammed shut as usual.

She was still trapped.

Without the third acorn, she would never be free.

Petrosinella had ripped her sleeve, crawling about looking for acorns. She didn't want the ogre to guess what she'd been doing, so she opened the ogre's sewing box, to stitch up her sleeve.

She heard something rattle in the bottom of the box. She tipped it upside down, and all the needles and pins and reels of thread fell out. The ogre's big thimble rattled loudly as it hit the floor. Petrosinella shook the thimble and out rolled the third acorn.

She dropped it into her pocket, beside the other two acorns.

Petrosinella grinned. 'I can escape, at last!'

'How will you climb down?' asked the prince. 'Everyone else uses your hair. Perhaps you should cut off your plait and tie it to the hook?'

'There's no need to cut off my hair.' Petrosinella sorted through the messy contents of the sewing box on the floor and knotted a ladder from the thread.

Petrosinella and the prince climbed out of the tower and down the ladder.

From the shadow of the trees, the nosy neighbour watched.

She wanted to bake apple crumble with apples from the wonderful garden, so she ran to the village market, found the tallest greenest customer, reached up high and tugged on the ogre's sleeve.

'She's escaped! Your girl in the tower climbed down with that boy and they're getting away!'

The ogre ran out of the market, still carrying her basket. She sprinted to the tower, roared her anger at the ladder dangling from the window, then followed the trail of footprints.

The ogre chased after Petrosinella and the prince as they ran through the forest. She had long legs and clawed feet and she ran twice as fast as the girl and the prince.

'When I catch you, Petrosinella,' shouted the ogre, 'I'll lock you in a smaller room in a taller tower and watch you fade away, like flowers always fade. When I catch your prince, I'll throw him in my soup pot!'

The prince turned pale, but Petrosinella said, 'Don't worry, she won't catch us.'

Petrosinella took the acorns from her pocket and spoke to them. 'Dearest acorns, powerful acorns, enchanted acorns, your lovely strong magic has been trapped in that tower for years, just like me. Please help me escape from the monster who trapped us all.'

Petrosinella threw the first acorn over her shoulder. It tumbled through the air and hit the ground behind her. The acorn bounced and rolled, and when it stopped, it turned into a big brown bear.

The bear snarled and clawed at the ogre, blocking her path.

The ogre put her hand in her basket, pulled out a spicy sausage she'd bought at market and threw it towards the bear.

The bear chewed at the sausage, and while it was distracted, the ogre ran past.

'When I catch you, Petrosinella,' she yelled, 'I'll shut you in a tower and watch you fade, then I'll eat your prince.'

The prince gasped, but Petrosinella said, 'Don't worry, she won't catch us.'

Petrosinella threw the second acorn over her shoulder. It tumbled through the air and hit the ground behind her. The acorn bounced and rolled, and when it stopped, it turned into a huge golden lion.

The lion roared and bit at the ogre, blocking her path.

The ogre grinned. She knew how to get past this lion. She put her hand in her basket, pulled out a thick slice of ham and threw it towards the lion.

The lion ripped at the ham, and while it was distracted, the ogre ran past.

'When I catch you, Petrosinella,' she shouted, 'I'll brick you up in the coldest darkest tower I can build, and I'll grind your prince's bones into my parsley bed.'

The prince's feet faltered, but Petrosinella said, 'Don't worry, she won't catch us.'

Petrosinella threw the third acorn over her shoulder. It tumbled through the air and hit the ground behind her. The acorn bounced and rolled, and when it stopped, it turned into a giant grey wolf.

The wolf howled and growled at the ogre, looming over her, blocking her path.

The ogre grinned. She knew how to get past this giant wolf. She put her hand in her basket, pulled out a loaf of bread and threw it towards the wolf.

The wolf sniffed at the bread, snorted and shook its head, then stepped over the loaf towards the ogre.

And the massive grey wolf opened its gigantic fanged jaws and swallowed the ogre, in one big gulp.

So Petrosinella and the prince stopped running through the forest and started walking.

The prince asked Petrosinella if she'd like to walk with him to his palace.

She smiled. 'No, thank you. When I was trapped in that tower, I thought I'd never see the world outside the forest; now I'm free, I don't want to stay in just one place.'

Then the girl who grew up in a tower went off to discover the world.

Every year, Petrosinella sent two postcards about her adventures, one to the prince in the palace by the dark forest and one to her mother in the house beside the beautiful garden.

But each year, that untended garden became more tangled, overgrown and filled with weeds.

FIRE AND RAIN

MEXICAN MYTH

Fire is our friend and fire is our enemy. Fire can provide warmth and light, fire can cook our food. Fire can also burn and kill.

Long ago, fire was neither friend nor enemy. Long ago, fire was entirely unknown.

Then, one day, a black rock cracked open and a tiny spark emerged. The spark perched on the edge of the crack. The next day, the spark danced in a circle on top of the rock. The day after that, the spark flew high in the air above the rock.

The people sent a girl and a boy, who were young enough to learn new things, to find out what the spark was.

'I am Fire,' said the spark. 'I can be your friend and I can be your enemy.'

The boy and the girl sat by the rock and spoke to Fire, hoping to make friends with him, so he would help their people.

Fire asked them to bring feathers to feed him and bowls to give him a safe home.

The girl and the boy brought Fire everything he asked for. He grew from a spark into a flame, and from one flame to many flames. As he grew, Fire became hot and beautiful, bright and glorious.

Fire asked for more to eat and burn. He asked for arrows, baskets, wax and beads. Full of all these good things, Fire became excited and wanted to eat more and more. Fire's flames leaped high and stretched far, and Fire started to burn everything he could reach.

The boy and the girl ran in fear from the fast and hungry flames.

Fire burned across the earth and burned through the air. Fire burned everything he touched. Fire roared his red-hot joy at the world around.

The people were terrified. They tried to drive Fire away. They threw wood at Fire, but he laughed and ate the wood. They threw rocks at him, but he laughed and melted the rocks.

Then the girl realised that Fire had asked for solid things to eat, but he had never asked for liquid to drink.

The girl shouted up to the sky, calling the name of the great goddess. 'Nakawé! Nakawé! Let down your hair!'

Nakawé looked down from the clouds and saw flames rushing over the land. She took off her hairnet, freeing her black plaited hair, and a few drops of water fell to Earth.

Fire hissed in disappointment.

Nakawé unplaited her hair, letting it swing loose, and drizzle fell to Earth.

Fire hissed angrily.

Nakawé brushed her hair and rain fell in heavy drops.

Fire began to shrink and steam.

Nakawé bent over and shook her hair above the earth, and a storm of water hit the ground.

Nakawé's storm doused Fire everywhere.

All except one tiny spark, hiding under an upturned bowl held by the boy and the girl.

Then Fire, sad and soggy and small, said sorry to the people. Fire suggested quietly that if they built a little clay house, he could live safely and calmly inside.

So the girl and the boy built a clay oven and put the spark inside. The spark grew into a comfortable size of fire, one that could cook and heat and light, but didn't hurt or burn or destroy.

Even now, fire can be your friend or fire can be your enemy. So it's wise to be cautious around sparks and flames. And it might also be wise to remember the name of the goddess Nakawé.

NANA MIRIAM AND
THE HUNGRY HIPPO

NIGERIAN LEGEND

This is the story of a girl who saved her village.

The villagers had always been wary of the hippos in the nearby River Niger. Despite their wide smiles and chubby tummies, hippos are fast and strong, with powerful jaws and bad tempers. Then, one night, the villagers saw a hippo that looked even more dangerous than ordinary hippos.

Because this hippo had just risen out of the river wearing fire.

This hippo was wearing an iron chain around his neck, with an iron pot dangling below his chin, and in the iron pot burned a bright red fire. The flames were burning strongly even as the hippo rose up through the water.

The villagers decided to leave this hippo alone.

But the hippo started to eat rice from the fields around the village.

The first night, he ate all the rice in one field. The next night, he ate all the rice in another field and trampled the plants into the ground. The third night, he ate all the rice in yet another field, trampled the plants and knocked down the fence.

If the hippo destroyed their whole crop, the villagers would starve. So despite their fear of this fiery hippo, the villagers fetched their sharpest metal tools. They stood close together and ran at the hippo, hoping to drive him away with yells and blades.

But when they struck the hippo, their blades bent and broke. The hippo's skin was hard as stone. No matter how loudly they yelled, or how bravely they attacked, the hippo ignored them.

The hippo just kept on eating their rice.

The villagers decided they needed help to deal with this invincible fiery hippo. They needed Fara Maka.

Fara Maka was the local magic-worker. In his youth he'd been a famous warrior, but now he spent his time teaching magic to his daughter Nana Miriam. He was teaching her how to discover the true names of things and how to use those names to draw on the power of everything around her.

When the villagers told Fara Maka about the fiery hippo and the threat to their crops, Fara Maka said to Nana Miriam, 'Lessons are over for today. I have to deal with a hippo.'

He grabbed his spear and walked towards the river.

Fara Maka's spear had won him many battles. The shaft contained all the weight and strength of an ancient tree; the blade contained all the sharpness and danger of a snake's fang.

Fara Maka aimed at the hippo's heart and threw his spear. The spear flew true through the air and struck the hippo in the perfect spot. But the spear bounced off the hippo's skin, clattered along the ground and slid to Fara Maka's feet.

Fara Maka looked surprised. The hippo didn't even look up.

Fara Maka decided he needed help to deal with this invincible fiery hippo. He needed dogs.

Fara Maka visited the local hunter and borrowed his pack of one hundred hunting hounds. Fara Maka hoped that while the ferocious fanged dogs distracted the hippo, he could attack the hippo's most vulnerable areas – eyes, ears, nostrils – and drive the hippo away.

He sent the hounds towards the hippo.

But this hippo wasn't just hungry for rice. The hippo snapped his jaws at the dogs, bit each dog in half, then swallowed each dog in two fast gulps.

One hundred snaps. Two hundred gulps. And the dogs were gone.

It wasn't the distraction Fara Maka had planned, but while the hippo was eating the hounds, Fara Maka got close enough to attack the hippo's face and ears with his spear.

The spear just bounced off. The hippo ignored him and went back to eating rice.

Fara Maka went home, sat down and put his head in his hands.

'What's wrong, Dad?' asked Nana Miriam.

Fara Maka told her about the hippo, the fire, the rice, the spear and the dogs. Then he said, 'I don't know what to do next.'

'Perhaps I can help,' said Nana Miriam.

'What could you do? I haven't taught you all my magic yet.'

'I could try different tactics. You're treating the hippo like an animal, attacking him with spears and dogs.'

'He *is* an animal!'

'Is he *just* an animal, though? He's got water-proof fire, spear-proof skin and a never-full belly, so I think the hippo has something magical trapped inside, something powerful and hungry. I'll speak to him as an equal, as one magic-user to another, and ask him politely to leave our village.'

Fara Maka shrugged. 'I suppose I have taught you to be polite.' He picked up his spear. 'I'll come and protect you.'

Nana Miriam shook her head. 'You've already annoyed the hippo, you should stay well back.'

As she left the house, she grabbed the belt she wore during her magic lessons, a belt with a dozen little bags dangling from it. She tied it round her waist and smiled at her dad. 'Just in case asking nicely doesn't work.'

Nana Miriam walked towards the river, with Fara Maka following at a distance.

She watched the hippo rise out of the water after a cooling dip and start eating the rice again.

Nana Miriam called out, 'Hello, hippo!'

The hippo ignored her.

She tried again. 'Hello, hippo! I've come to ask, as one magic-user to another: please do me the courtesy of leaving my village.'

The hippo ignored her.

Nana Miriam said, 'Hippo, please leave my village, or I will *make* you leave.'

The hippo finally looked up. At this little girl, with a silly belt round her waist, daring to threaten him!

The hippo laughed. As he laughed, he shook his big grey belly and all the drops of water on his shiny skin flew into the air.

The drops joined together to make a ring of water, which whirled over to Nana Miriam and dropped down around her.

Suddenly Nana Miriam was trapped inside a deep dark circle of water.

The hippo kept laughing.

But Nana Miriam just smiled. She reached into one of her little bags and took out a pinch of sawdust.

She whispered to the sawdust, then sprinkled it on the water. And that tiny pinch of sawdust soaked up all the water.

Nana Miriam walked three paces nearer the hippo, squelching over the damp earth with her bare toes. 'I'll ask again: hippo, please leave my village.'

The hippo blew a breath at her. The gust of air drew a flame from the pot below his jaws. The flame flew towards Nana Miriam, circled round her, then touched the ground and started to burn the grass at her feet.

Suddenly Nana Miriam was trapped inside a ring of flames higher than her head.

She could hear the hippo laughing.

Nana Miriam smiled, reached into one of her little bags and took out a pinch of soil.

She whispered to the soil, then threw it on the fire. And that tiny pinch of soil smothered all the flames.

Nana Miriam walked three more paces towards the hippo, scuffing the hot ash with her bare toes. 'Hippo, this is the last time I will ask politely. Please leave my village.'

The hippo bit down on the iron pot dangling below his jaws. As his teeth touched the metal, a ring of iron shot up out of the ground around Nana Miriam.

Suddenly Nana Miriam was trapped inside a high wall of metal.

She couldn't see the hippo, but she could hear him laughing.

Nana Miriam smiled, reached into one of her little bags and took out a tiny hammer.

She whispered to the hammer, reached up high and tapped the metal wall.

Clink...

The metal wall shattered into thousands of shining fragments. Nana Miriam stepped carefully through them, avoiding the sharp edges with her bare toes.

She called out, 'I've been polite to you, though you haven't been even slightly polite to me. Now I'm just going to tell you to GET OUT OF MY VILLAGE!'

The hippo stared at this small girl, with her silly belt. And he didn't laugh.

Could this little girl drive him away? He'd tried to defeat her with water, fire and iron, but she was still there, still shouting at him.

Perhaps she *could* drive him away!

The hippo looked past Nana Miriam. In the distance he saw Fara Maka, standing watching with his spear in his hand.

The hippo thought if he couldn't defeat this girl with water, fire or iron, perhaps he could defeat her by harming someone she loved. So the hippo started to charge, not straight at Nana Miriam, but at an angle, towards Fara Maka.

Nana Miriam watched this fast heavy vicious animal run towards her dad, who had only his spear to protect him. A spear that had already failed against this hippo.

Nana Miriam dug her bare toes into the earth. She whispered the most powerful name she knew. She drew up as much strength as she could from the land.

When the hippo charged past her, Nana Miriam reached out and grabbed his tail.

She lifted the hippo into the air, she whirled the hippo round her head and she threw the hippo away.

The hippo with the fiery necklace flew over the rice fields, over the village, over the river and far, far away. The hippo hit the ground a whole year's journey away from Nana Miriam's village.

I don't know whether the thump when the hippo hit the ground knocked the hungry magic right out of him. But I do know that ever since that day no hippo, magical or not, has dared to eat even one grain of rice from Nana Miriam's village.

MARIA AND
THE CONDOR

ECUADORIAN FOLK TALE

Maria lived on a small farm by a wide river, with her granny, her little brother and her little sister.

Once a year, the river rose above its banks and flooded. Most years, the floods were low and slow and welcome, because they made the fields rich and fertile. But some years, when the winter snows were heavy and spring arrived suddenly, the floods could be high and fast and dangerous.

In those years, local families ran to the mountains, to escape the floodwaters.

One morning, Maria's granny shouted, 'The river's rising fast! Pack your bags, we have to leave!'

Maria and her little brother and her little sister each packed a loaf of bread, a knife and a blanket, then threw their bags on their backs and followed their granny out of the house.

As she left, Maria saw a little spider spinning a silvery web in the corner of the doorframe.

'Oh, clever spider,' said Maria. 'That's a beautiful web, but you won't get a chance to finish it. There's a flood coming, you should scuttle away to safety!' She waved at the spider and the spider waved back with its two front legs.

Maria ran after her granny, her brother and her sister, with the rumble and roar of the flood behind her. When she caught up with them, they were arguing about the best way to reach the safety of the mountains.

Maria didn't join in the argument, because she'd just noticed a large heap of jagged black feathers slumped behind a fence. She looked over the fence.

The heap of feathers was a condor, the huge soaring bird of the high mountains, with hooked beak, white ruff and massive wide black wings. But this condor wasn't spreading his wings, he was hunched on the ground, muttering and grumbling.

'Oh, majestic condor,' said Maria. 'There's a flood coming, you should fly away to safety!'

The condor snapped, 'I can't fly away, you stupid girl. Look at my feet.'

Maria looked down. His huge taloned feet were trapped in a snare. She used her knife to slice through the snare.

The condor spread his wide wings and flew into the air. 'Why did you do that?' he asked, as he circled above Maria.

'I didn't want you to drown in the flood.'

'I suppose I should repay you for saving me,' said the condor. 'I will give you the traditional three favours. You may whistle for me three times and three times only, and each time I will grant you one favour.'

The condor soared up towards the high peaks.

Maria felt the ground rumble under her feet and heard the roar of the flood getting closer, so she ran to catch up with her family, who had finally stopped arguing about the best way to safety.

But they'd agreed on the wrong path. Because soon Maria and her family stood at the foot of a cliff. They'd missed the turn-off to the gentle slopes, and followed a path to the base of a high rock face instead.

The floodwaters were rushing towards them. There was no time to retrace their steps and find the other path. They had to reach the top of the cliff.

So Maria, her granny, her little sister and her little brother all tried to climb the rock face. But it was impossible. There were no handholds, no footholds.

Now the flood was so close they could smell the water in the air and feel the earth shaking under their feet.

Maria looked at her family. Her granny, her sister, her brother.

Three people.

And Maria was owed three favours.

So she whistled.

The condor soared down on his wide wings. 'Do you want a favour already?'

'Yes, please lift my granny to the top of the cliff.'

The condor grabbed the straps of her granny's bag in his talons and flew her to the top of the cliff. He dropped the old woman on the hard ground with a thump.

Maria's granny was now safe, high above the approaching flood.

The condor started to fly away.

Maria whistled again.

The condor soared down on his wide wings. 'Do you want another favour already?'

'Yes, please lift my little sister to the top of the cliff.'

The condor grabbed the straps of her sister's bag in his talons and flew her to the top of the cliff. He dropped the little girl on the hard ground with a thump. Maria's sister was now safe, high above the approaching flood.

The condor started to fly away.

Maria whistled again.

The condor soared down on his wide wings. 'Do you want another favour already?'

'Yes, please lift my brother to the top of the cliff.'

The condor circled above her. 'Can't you count, stupid girl? I gave you three favours. You have already used two favours. Therefore you only have one favour left. This is your last favour. Your last chance. Why would you waste it on someone else?'

Maria looked at her little brother, pressed against the cliff, pale-faced with fear. She looked at the brown waters rushing towards them both.

Maria nodded. 'I know this is my last favour and I also know that saving my brother is not a waste. Please lift him to the top of the cliff.'

The condor grabbed the straps of her brother's bag in his talons and flew him to the top of the cliff. He dropped the little boy on the hard ground with a thump. Maria's brother was now safe, high above the approaching flood.

The condor started to fly away.

Maria thought: I saved the condor out of kindness, with no promise of reward, so maybe he'll save me out of kindness too.

She whistled.

The condor kept flying away.

Maria whistled again.

The floodwaters arrived. The brown rushing water crashed against her legs and shoved her against the rock face.

She whistled again.

But the condor was just a black smudge in the distance.

The condor wasn't coming back.

Maria looked up at her family, peering over the edge of the cliff. She looked down at the floodwater, rising higher and higher.

'I'll just have to save myself,' said Maria.

So she started to climb.

She found cracks in the rock almost deep enough for her fingernails. She found bumps in the rock almost wide enough for her toes.

She tried to climb the cliff. But her nails broke, and the rock was wet and slippy from the splashing floodwaters below.

Maria slid off and fell into the rising flood.

The water was deep and cold. The force of the flood battered her against the rock, then tried to drag her away from the cliff.

Maria found a desperate burst of energy, hauled herself out and clung to the rock. She started to climb the cliff again.

But now she was shivering with cold and trembling with fear. She slipped slowly down the cliff again, towards the fast floodwaters.

Then she saw a silvery rope snake down the rock face towards her.

Just before her toes touched the water, her fingers grabbed the rope.

Maria used the silky soft slightly sticky rope to climb up and up, away from the cold flood.

Finally, she reached the top of the rope and the top of the cliff. Her granny and sister and brother pulled her to safety.

On the cliff edge, beside the silvery silky rope, Maria saw a little spider. The spider waved its two front legs. Maria waved back. 'Thanks for spinning me a cobweb rope!'

For two days, the family watched the floodwaters rise higher and higher, covering all the land they knew. For two more days, they watched the waters fall, until they could see houses and fields again.

They found the gentle sloping path down the mountain and walked back home. They dried and repaired their house, and planted seeds in their rich wet fields.

For the rest of Maria's long life, she was always happy to let spiders build webs in the corners of her house. But she never invited any condors round for tea.

THE LACE DRAGON

CHINESE FOLK TALE

Once upon a time, in a small village near the mountains, there was a young lace-maker who worked with such skill and passion that her lace looked almost, but not quite, alive.

Her lace flowers looked as if they were about to blow in a breeze and grow; her lace animals looked as if they were about to take a breath and move. When her family and friends wore her perfect lace, they felt surrounded by beauty, life and happiness, so they called her Sister Lace.

She started to teach lace-making to other young women, hoping they could all sell their lace at faraway markets, so their whole village could become prosperous.

The Chinese emperor heard of her wonderful lace and sent his guards to fetch the young lace-maker. Sister Lace didn't want to leave her village, but the guards said they would drag her to the palace if she didn't go willingly. So she packed her sharpest pins and bobbins of her finest thread, and said to her keen pupils, 'I'll be back soon.'

When she arrived at the palace, the emperor said, 'I've heard of your marvellous lace: the way the flowers seem to grow and the animals seem to breathe. I want that beauty all for myself. You will marry me, stay in my palace forever and make lace only for me.'

Sister Lace didn't want to stay in the palace, she wanted to go back to her village and share her skills. She didn't want to make lace only for the emperor, she wanted everyone to enjoy her lace. And she really didn't want to marry this selfish demanding man.

She said politely, 'No thank you, Your Majesty. I would prefer to return to my village and make lace with my friends and family.'

'How dare you refuse me?' The emperor turned to his guards. 'Throw her in prison! Take her pins and thread away. Feed her on old rice and stagnant water. That will make her change her mind!'

But Sister Lace didn't change her mind. Every day the emperor visited her cell, to demand that she marry him, stay in his palace and make lace only for him. Every day she refused.

Eventually he said, 'I will give you one chance to go home to your village. I will set you a lace-making test and if you pass I will set you free. But first you have to agree that if you fail, you will marry me.'

Sister Lace was keen to go home and was confident of her lace-making skills, so she agreed.

The emperor grinned. 'Then by tomorrow morning, you must make me a real live mouse of lace!' He tossed her bobbins and pins through the bars.

Sister Lace worked all night to make a perfect life-sized mouse, with ears and nose and tiny little paws. When the sun came up, she pricked herself deliberately with a pin and let one drop of her blood fall into the lacy eye of the mouse.

The delicate little mouse began to move. It scurried around the cell, sniffing the corners and nibbling the dry rice. When the emperor arrived, the pink-eyed white mouse was running happily around the lace-maker's feet.

'A mouse of lace,' said Sister Lace, 'as you requested.'

'But... but... but... that's impossible!' he shouted. 'That moving mouse can't be made from lace, it must have crept in through a hole in the wall. You must try again. By tomorrow morning, you must make me a real live cockerel of lace.'

Sister Lace worked all night to make a perfect life-sized cockerel, with feathers, beak and high confident tail. When the sun came up, she pricked herself deliberately with a pin and let one drop of her blood fall into the lacy eye of the cockerel.

The proud white bird began to move. It strutted around the cell, flapping its wings. When the emperor arrived, the white cockerel crowed.

'Cock a doodle doo!'

'A cockerel of lace,' said Sister Lace, 'as you requested.'

'But... but... but... that's impossible!' he shouted. 'That crowing cockerel can't be made from lace, it must have flown in the window. You must try again and this time you must create a beast that can't possibly get into your cell any other way. By tomorrow morning, you must make me a real live *dragon* of lace.'

Sister Lace worked as fast as she had ever worked, to make a life-sized dragon, with sharp horns, long claws, wide wings and powerful jaws. By the time she was finished, the coils of the lace dragon covered the floor of the cell.

When the sun came up, she pricked herself deliberately with a pin and let one drop of her blood fall into the lacy eye of the dragon.

The huge sinuous dragon began to move. It twisted and stretched, filling the cell with its tail and wings and jaws, pushing the lace-maker, the mouse and the cockerel into one corner.

When the emperor arrived, sure she must have failed, sure she would have to marry him now, he saw a dragon in the cell.

'A dragon of lace,' said Sister Lace, 'as you requested.'

This dragon was obviously made of lace: the emperor could see intricate lacy patterns on every scale. It was obviously alive: moving and breathing and pushing against the bars. And there was no other way a dragon could have got into the cell.

But if the emperor admitted that his prisoner had made a live dragon of lace, he would have to set her free. So he said, 'That's not what I asked for, that's not a dragon, that's just... that's just... that's just a big fat snake!'

Dragons do not like being called snakes. Especially not big fat snakes.

The lace dragon stared at the emperor, with its blood-red eyes set in pure-white scales, and it blasted a ball of fire at him.

The lace dragon burned the emperor where he stood.

The lace dragon burned down the prison and the palace.

Then the lace dragon leaped from the ashes and flew away, with Sister Lace, the delicate mouse and the proud cockerel sitting on its back.

The dragon flew the cockerel, the mouse and Sister Lace to her village. The mouse made a nest in Sister Lace's bobbin box, the cockerel bossed the local hens about, and Sister Lace taught a whole generation of talented lace-makers, so their village became famous and prosperous.

Sister Lace continued to make lace for her family and friends, and that lace was so beautiful it looked almost alive. Almost, but not quite. Because she was far too skilled to prick her finger and drip blood on her lace by accident.

And the lace dragon, pure-white with blood-red eyes, flew to the mountains and lived on the highest peak. Almost, but not quite, hidden in the snow and ice...

ALTYN ARYG AND THE
SNAKE'S BELLY

SIBERIAN LEGEND

Once there was a khan who led the largest tribe in Siberia. He described himself as an unfortunate man, because he had no sons. But the unfortunate person was really his one daughter, Altyn Aryg, because the khan never stopped moaning about how much happier he would be if he had a son instead of a daughter.

It didn't matter how hard Altyn Aryg trained to become the tribe's fiercest warrior, most skilled horse-rider and strongest sword-fighter. Her father just kept saying, 'But who will lead the tribe after me? How unfortunate I am to have no worthy heir...'

It didn't matter how many lost lambs or calves Altyn Aryg found and returned to the herd, nor how many tribal disputes she resolved with wisdom and diplomacy, nor how many thieves she tracked and caught. Her father still kept saying, 'Even one hundred girls wouldn't be equal to one boy...'

Eventually Altyn Aryg realised that her father would never be impressed with mere human deeds. She needed to do something superhuman.

She said to her father, 'I will show you what one girl can do!' Then she grabbed his favourite sword and marched out of the tent to hunt for a snake.

She wasn't hunting for an ordinary snake; she was hunting for the giant snake that had been terrorising Siberia for years.

This snake was so enormous that a horse would take a day to gallop along its spine and a tribe could pitch fifty tents in a line across its neck. Its fangs were longer than ten men are tall, and its mouth was wide enough to swallow a tribe in one gulp.

The monstrous snake demanded that each tribe pay tribute of one thousand cattle a year. If any tribe refused, the snake ate the whole tribe. In one gulp.

When khans ordered heroes to defeat the snake, the snake devoured the heroes too.

Altyn Aryg hoped that if she could defeat the snake, her father would finally respect her.

She tracked the monster, following the trail of crushed plants, cracked earth and weeping relatives. She found a snake as long as a river, as high as a hill, with a grass-green belly and a sky-blue back.

Altyn Aryg rode all the way up to the monstrous head, jumped off her exhausted horse and stood in front of the snake.

'Have you come to pay me tribute?' asked the snake.

'Why would I pay tribute to a monster? You don't deserve my respect or my tribute.'

'Then I will eat you.' The snake opened its massive mouth.

'No need to eat me,' replied Altyn Aryg. 'I'll jump right in!'

And she did. The khan's daughter leaped between the snake's fangs into the snake's mouth. She ran down the snake's throat, towards the snake's belly.

And the snake's jaws snapped shut behind her.

Altyn Aryg looked around the long belly, which was full of people, their animals, their tents and their lamps.

The snake's digestive juices worked slowly, so while there were many gently dissolving corpses at the far end of the belly, there were also herds of cattle, tribes of people and one hundred heroes, all sitting sadly at the other end, waiting to die.

Altyn Aryg marched up to the one hundred heroes and said, 'I'm here to help.'

'No one can help,' said one of the swallowed heroes. 'There's no way to escape and no way to kill this beast.' He pointed to the left side of the belly. 'Its heart is so hard, none of us can pierce it.'

Altyn Aryg said, 'Give me your swords!'

The heroes handed her their one hundred swords, then she stabbed and slashed at the heart. It was like hitting a rock, and she couldn't pierce it either. However Altyn Aryg was so strong that every sword she swung against the snake's solid heart shattered into a dozen pieces.

Finally she only had one sword left: her father's favourite sword.

She looked closely at the snake's heart. In the place she'd been striking, the spot where she'd already broken one hundred swords, there was one hairline crack.

She aimed at the tiny wound, she lunged forward with all her strength...

And Altyn Aryg drove the sword deep into the snake's heart.

She dragged the blade out. The snake's black blood oozed on to her hands.

The snake gasped and shuddered, and its mouth fell open.

Altyn Aryg led the tribes, the herds and the heroes out of the snake's belly and out of its open mouth. They stood together and watched the snake writhe and die.

The tribes thanked Altyn Aryg. 'You have defeated the monster and set us all free. We will pay tribute to you now.'

Altyn Aryg shook her head. 'You may keep your herds.'

'But you've done what one hundred heroes couldn't do! You can't go home empty-handed.'

She smiled. 'Once I tell my father how the snake died, my hands won't be empty for long.'

Altyn Aryg rode back to her father's tent, and she told him about the snake, the one hundred shattered swords and the pierced heart. She showed him the black blood on his sword and on her hands.

The khan bowed his head to Altyn Aryg. 'You have done what one hundred sons could not have done.'

Finally, the khan named his one and only daughter Altyn Aryg as his heir, and he offered her both his favourite sword and his respect.

FINDING OUR OWN HEROINES

I'm sure all the readers of this book know that girls and boys are equal and should be allowed – in real life and in stories – to defeat their own monsters, go on their own quests, make their own mistakes and solve their own problems. But unfortunately not everyone acts as if that were true, so there is still a need for stories which show that girls are and *always have been* just as capable, strong, brave and smart as boys.

Just like the stories in *Girls, Goddesses & Giants*, my first collection of heroine myths and legends, these stories are all genuine traditional tales. I've not turned any heroes into heroines, or male warriors into female ones. I've not taken a story about a boy doing something amazing, then stuck a girl in the lead role instead, just to make a point. These tales have all been told, for many years, in many places, about girls who are the stars of their own stories, rather than sidekicks or prizes. (Girls have starred in stories for as long as stories have been told: the story of the goddess who wrestled a mountain is well over four thousand years old.)

However, I have made other changes to the stories, as every storyteller does. When I share these stories, with live audiences or in print, I tell them in my own voice and in my own way, which is never exactly the way I first heard or read them.

One change that I've made to several of these stories is to cancel the wedding at the end. I've always done this when telling stories out loud, and I used to think I was making a major and radical change to the plot. But recently I've wondered whether the 'happy ever after' ending may have been stuck on to some stories because it was the easiest way to end them. Finding the right line to end a story can be really hard, and once upon a time a storyteller might have thought, 'I've no idea what to do now the girl has defeated the monster! I'll just say she married a prince and lived happily ever after, then everyone will know the story has ended...' If a story is about someone searching for the love of their life, the 'marrying a handsome prince' ending might make sense; if the story is about a girl escaping an ogre, a 'marriage' ending isn't necessary to the plot and might not have been part of the original story. (We'll never know, because most traditional tales weren't written down until relatively recently.) So I've removed those unnecessary weddings and let the girls decide their own futures...

I'd like you to be able to track these heroines back a few steps, so here's information about where I found each story. I hope you enjoy discovering more about the stories and the people who first told them, and possibly retelling them yourself, in your own way!

KANDEK AND THE WOLF

Armenian Folk Tale

There aren't many female werewolves in folklore, and even fewer elderly werewolves. So, unlike Kandek, I was delighted to meet this hungry old wolf! I found the story in *Armenian Folk-tales and Fables* by Charles Downing (Oxford University Press, 1972).

GODDESS VS MOUNTAIN

Sumerian Myth

This was the first Inanna story I ever told, when my frustration at the lack of strong heroines in classical mythology prompted a university lecturer friend to suggest that I look further back in time, at the stories hidden for thousands of years under the sands of Iraq, to find a really kickass goddess. I've been an Inanna fan ever since. I've worked with various translations of this mountain-wrestling myth, but it was Betty de Shong Meador's *Inanna, Lady of Largest Heart* (University of Texas Press, 2000) that encouraged me to imagine Ebih as a volcano.

NERINGA AND
THE SEA DRAGON

Lithuanian Legend

There are stories all over the world about giants creating the local landscape, often when they're fighting each other, so it's unusual and wonderful that Neringa built this sandy peninsula to protect the people she loved. I first discovered Neringa in *The Atlas of Monsters* by Sandra Lawrence and Stuart Hill (Big Picture Press, 2017) then pieced together her story from various tourist publications, travel blogs and websites.

KATE CRACKERNUTS AND THE SHEEP-HEADED MONSTER

Scottish Fairy Tale

This is one of my favourite Scottish fairy tales, partly because of that grotesque sheep's head, but mainly because the two stepsisters love each other, which doesn't happen nearly often enough in stories. There are lots of versions of Kate's story, but I first found this tale in *The Mermaid Bride* by Tom Muir (The Orcadian Ltd, 1998).

RIINA AND THE RED STONE AXE

Solomon Islands Folk Tale

I was drawn to this story not just by the boat full of warrior women, but also because Riina defeated the cannibal by breaking a taboo. Breaking rules is often punished in traditional tales, but this is a wonderful example of how breaking rules can give you power. I found this Solomon Islands story in *Pacific Island Legends* by Bo Flood, Beret Strong and William Flood (Bess Press, 1999).

MEDEA AND
THE METAL MAN

Greek Myth

Medea gets a bad press (she does some horrible things in other stories) but she is a heroine in this tale, using her cleverness and courage to defeat Talos. As with any Greek myth there are as many versions as grains of sand on a Cretan beach, but my starting point for this retelling was *Tales of the Greek Heroes* by Roger Lancelyn Green (Penguin Books, 1958).

BRIDGET AND THE WITCHES

Irish Folk Tale

This story is told in slightly different forms in my own country of Scotland, so I was intrigued to find this version in *Irish Folktales*, edited by Henry Glassie (Pantheon Books, 1985). I'm not a big fan of housework (reading books and sharing stories are always more urgent) and I'm relieved to say that, despite my untidy house, I've never been bothered by witches spinning beside my fireplace.

PETROSINELLA AND THE TOWER

Italian Fairy Tale

This story reminds me that any well-known fairy tale, like Rapunzel, is just one version of a tale which has been told in many different ways in many different cultures. I particularly like this 'girl with long hair trapped in a tower' tale because she manages to escape using magic and because it has a wonderful chase scene. (When I tell it to audiences, I usually end up crawling around on the floor looking for those acorns. It's a glamorous job, being a storyteller...) I found Petrosinella in *The Tale of Tales* by Giambattista Basile, originally written in the seventeenth century (translated by Nancy Canepa, Wayne State University Press, 2007).

FIRE AND RAIN

Mexican Myth

Many cultures tell stories about how humans first got access to fire, often about a bird bringing fire to earth. I like this very different fire origin story, from the Wixárika people of Mexico, because it recognises how dangerous fire can be and gives fire a personality. Also, I love the image of the goddess brushing raindrops out of her hair. There's a more detailed version in *Huichol Mythology* by Robert Zingg (University of Arizona Press, 2004).

NANA MIRIAM AND THE HUNGRY HIPPO

Nigerian Legend

I love stories about magical apprentices outdoing their teachers, and it's even better when a daughter shows her dad how to defeat a monster! The story of how Nana Miriam defeated the hippo is told by the Songhai people in the lands by the River Niger. I found it in *West African Folktales* by Steven Gale (NTC Publishing, 1995) and it has become one of my favourite stories to tell when I visit schools.

MARIA AND THE CONDOR

Ecuadorian Folk Tale

I didn't find this story in a book: it reached me in a much more interesting way. I was mentoring a wonderful young Scottish storyteller called Ailsa Dixon, and during the time we were working together, she went on an international scout camp, where she asked her fellow scouts if they knew folk tales from their own countries. Two Ecuadorian girls called Sara and Adriana told her this story, then she told the story to me, and now I've told the story to you. That's how stories have always travelled the world. (It's also how they change, because Ailsa and I tell the story slightly differently!) Thanks so much to Ailsa, Sara and Adriana.

THE LACE DRAGON

Chinese Folk Tale

Many stories about strong, brave and clever girls involve spinning or sewing, so I was delighted to find a story where a girl's skill with thread drags her into a drama with an emperor, a palace and that beautiful terrifying lacy dragon. I found this story in *The Moon Maiden and Other Asian Folktales* by the Hua Long collective (China Books, San Francisco, 1993). I admit that I invented the lacy mouse; it was a partridge in the source story, but once I'd imagined a delicate lacy mouse, I couldn't tell it any other way!

ALTYN ARYG AND THE SNAKE'S BELLY

Siberian Legend

When the stories in this book were first told, none of these heroines would have described themselves as feminists, because the word didn't exist. But Altyn Aryg definitely had to battle against sexism and use all her girl power to impress her dad. He was probably more difficult to deal with than the huge snake... I found this story in the *Encyclopaedia of Folk Heroes* by Graham Seal (ABC-CLIO, 2001).

ABOUT THE AUTHOR

Lari Don

Lari is an award-winning writer for young people of all ages. She loved traditional tales and folklore as a child, and now collects stories of any shape and size, from all sorts of sources, to inspire her novels. *Fierce, Fearless and Free* is her fifth anthology for Bloomsbury, returning to the theme of her first – the best-selling *Girls, Goddesses and Giants*. She lives in Edinburgh with her husband and two fierce, fearless and free daughters.

ABOUT THE ILLUSTRATOR

Eilidh Muldoon

When Eilidh isn't drawing she's thinking about drawing and she loves nothing more than to immerse herself in the world of traditional stories. Her sketch books are packed with detailed drawings and plots and plans. An illustrator and designer, she loves the variety of working one day on one of her popular colouring books or city-scape prints, and the next on one of Lari's extraordinary heroines. *Fierce, Fearless and Free* is her first book for Bloomsbury.

Also by
LARI DON

ISBN: 9781408188224

A selection of brilliant folk tales about heroines from all around the world. In these stories it's the girls who save the day through their courage, cunning or kindness – whether they are facing up to wolves, demons, dragons, enemy tribes or the sun itself! Handsome princes need not apply – these girls are doing it for themselves.

Also by
LARI DON

ISBN: 9781472920973

Have you ever heard of the horse who had gold in his dung, or of the Fire Horse of Hiisi with his mane of gold and red flame and smouldering black hooves? What about the hippogriff, the centaurs and the wise colt?

This is a collection of stories about warriors, monsters and heroes' horses and about the origins of horses and people. It is an anthology of stories where horses are magical and stories where horses are the villains; perfect for any horse lover.

Also by
LARI DON

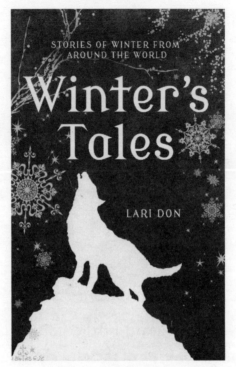

ISBN: 9781472900166

A selection of folk tales about winter from all around the world. Find out how spiders invented tinsel, what happened when the spring girl beat the hag of winter, why snow is eagles' feathers, and how a hero with hairy trousers used ice to kill a dragon.